For Mr. Bunny

Published by
Princeton Architectural Press
202 Warren Street
Hudson, New York 12534
www.papress.com

First published in Canada under the title *Pleine Lune*
Copyright © 2019, Comme des géants, Varennes, Canada

English edition © 2021 Princeton Architectural Press
This edition was published by arrangement with
The Picture Book Agency, France.
All rights reserved.
Printed and bound in China
24 23 22 21 4 3 2 1 First edition

ISBN 978-1-61689-999-8

Editor: Stephanie Holstein
Typesetting: Natalie Snodgrass

Library of Congress Control Number: 2020940855

FULL
MOON

Camilla Pintonato

PRINCETON ARCHITECTURAL PRESS · NEW YORK

In the quiet forest, the rabbits hide,

eagerly waiting for the sun to set.

One sticks out its little nose. Is it dark yet?

Five little gray rabbits hop out of their burrow
and set out on a journey into the night.

Where are they going?

What are they carrying in their backpacks?

Something round, bright, and beautiful.

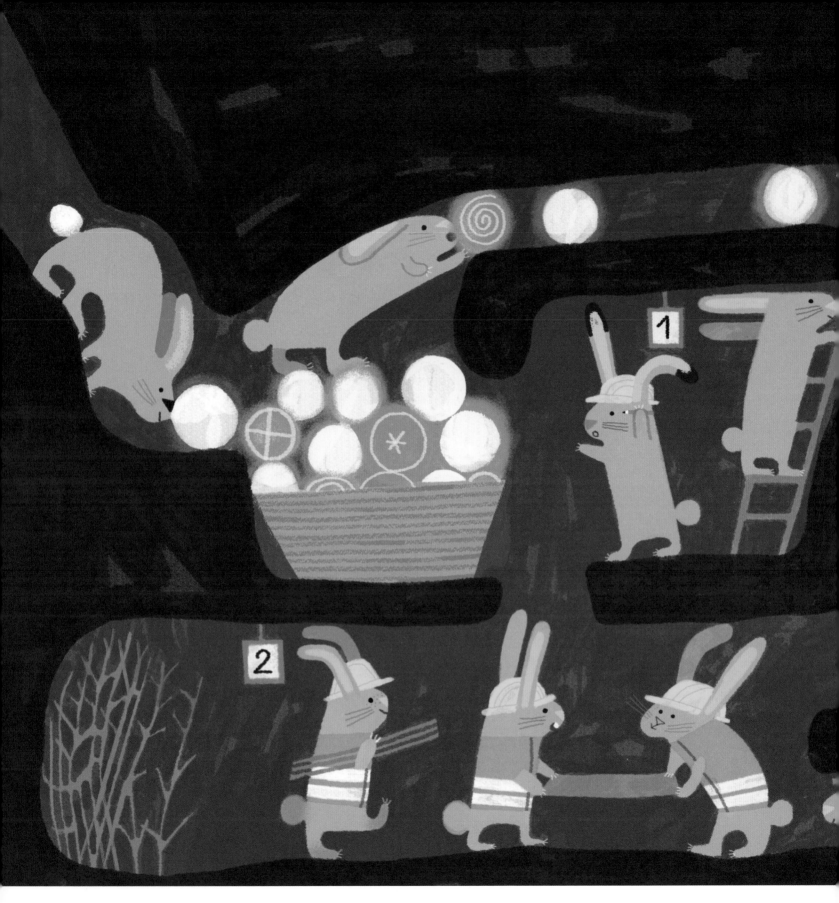

In their secret workshop, the rabbits are very busy!

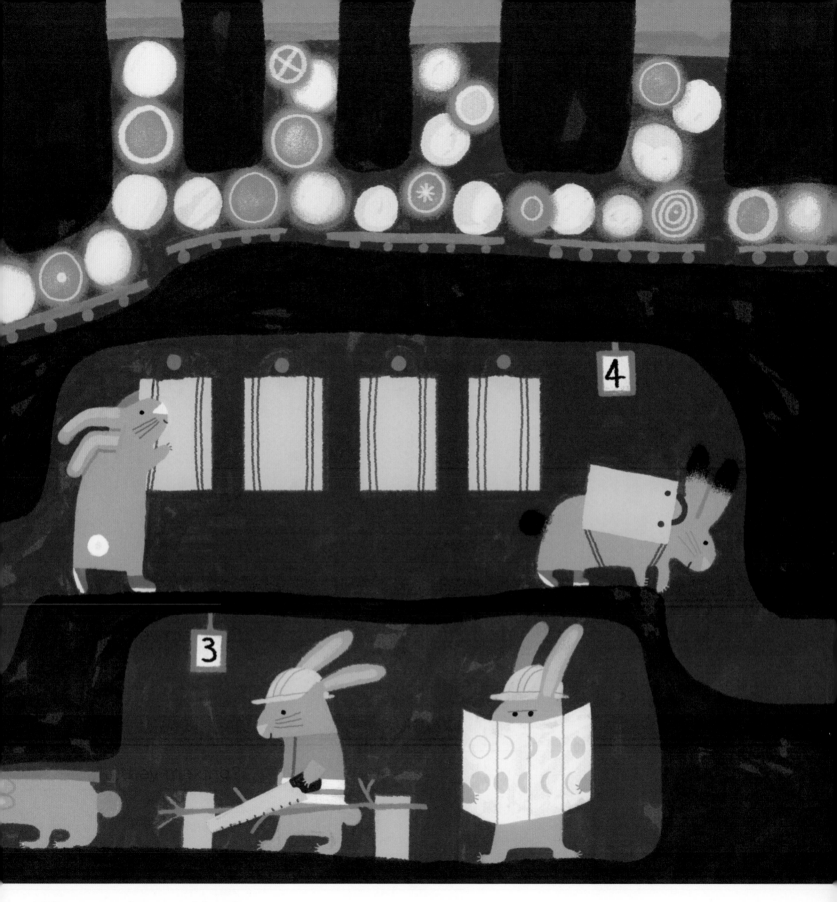

What are they making?

Eagerly waiting for the moon to rise,

the little gray rabbits print, cut, and stack,
preparing for a celebration.

Now what are they carrying in their backpacks?
A drawing, a letter, an invitation?

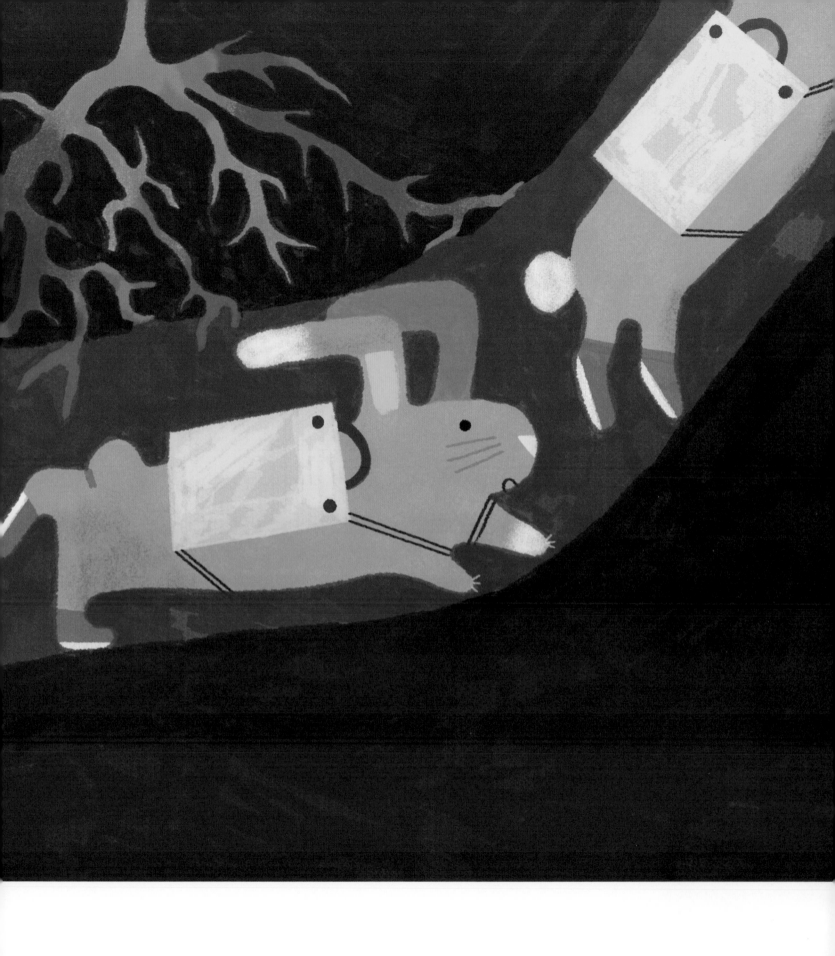

Feathered friends, please join us!
There is a full moon tonight.

Mouse family, please join us for the big event!

Everyone is invited.

Soon the moon is high in the sky!

The guests follow the rabbits through the forest
to gather together underneath the stars.

The rabbits show them where to sit for the big surprise.

Places!

Wait!

Ready?

GO!

As the birds begin to sing, the lanterns lift up into the sky.

The little gray rabbits and their friends are dazzled by the light.

Before their eyes, the full moon shines bright.

The paper lanterns sparkle like stars.

When the show is over, the creatures scurry home to dream of the moon and the stars and the lanterns setting the night sky aglow.

The full moon sets and gives way to the sun.

And in their cozy burrow, the little gray rabbits have hidden themselves once again, awaiting the next full moon celebration.

Will you join them?